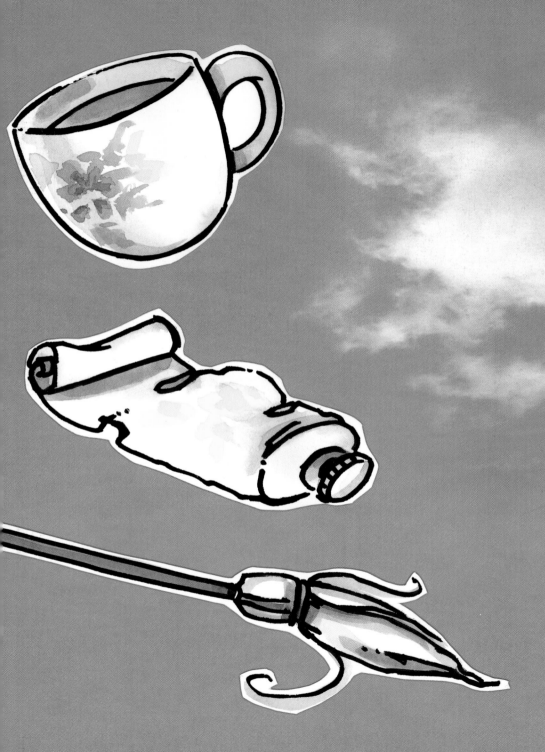

How to Make a Night

By Linda Ashman • Illustrated by Tricia Tusa

HARPERCOLLINSPUBLISHERS

To Lou and Betty Schaefer, and, as always,
to Jackson, with love
—L.A.

For Rhe and Horsie
—T.T.

How to Make a Night
Text copyright © 2004 by Linda Ashman
Illustrations copyright © 2004 by Tricia Tusa
Manufactured in China by South China Printing Company Ltd.
www.harperchildrens.com

Library of Congress Cataloging-in-Publication Data
Ashman, Linda.
How to make a night / by Linda Ashman ; illustrated by Tricia Tusa.
    p.   cm.
Summary: After a hectic day, it is time to bring on the night so that a child
and her family can finally rest.
ISBN 0-06-029032-3 — ISBN 0-06-029014-5 (lib. bdg.)
[1. Bedtime—Fiction.   2. Night—Fiction.   3. Stories in rhyme.]
I. Tusa, Tricia, ill.   II. Title.
PZ8.3.A775Ho 2004   [E]—dc21   2002010502

Typography by Elynn Cohen   1 2 3 4 5 6 7 8 9 10   ❖   First Edition

How to Make a Night

Bike blew a tire.

Boat sprang a leak.

Scooter's in the gutter.

Sneaker's in the creek.

Train skipped the track.
Cat spilled the juice.
Cake's on the floor.
Snake's on the loose.

Papa's hair is haywire.
Mama's face is pale.

Pup is in the corner with his head
beneath his tail.

Time to settle down!
Time to clean the mess!
Time to bring the night around
so everyone can rest.

Slip away.
Get to work.
Climb a tree
to the top.

Clear the clouds from the sky
with a big, wet mop.

Find a rope.

Make a loop.
Let it loose in space.

Catch the sun.
Pull it down.

Find a safe, dark place.

Peel the blue from the sky.
Squirt some dye in a sink.
Dunk the blue in the dye 'til
it's black like ink.

Shake it out. Get some paint.
Splatter gold on the black.
There's your bright starry night. Lift it up.
Throw it back.

Find a big yellow rock.
Rub it smooth.
Make a moon.

Fling the stone into space
with a long silver spoon.

Call the owls! Call the crickets!
Let the night chorus sing!

Stir the wind 'til it whistles
and the treetops swing.

Climb a hill.
Look around. What a sky! What a view! It's a fine, fine night—

but you're not quite through.

Tumble down. Hurry home.
Toss your toys into place.
Clean your room 'til it shines.
Wash your hands.
Scrub your face.

Find your family.
Eat your supper.
Take a bath. Comb your hair.

Choose a pair of soft pajamas.
Grab your best old bear.
Let your papa give you kisses.
Let your mama hold you tight.
Burrow down beneath your blankets.
Snuggle in and say good night.

Close your eyes and slumber soundly.
You'll be busy very soon . . .

when it's time to toss the sun up high
and haul away the moon.